PEACE CRANE

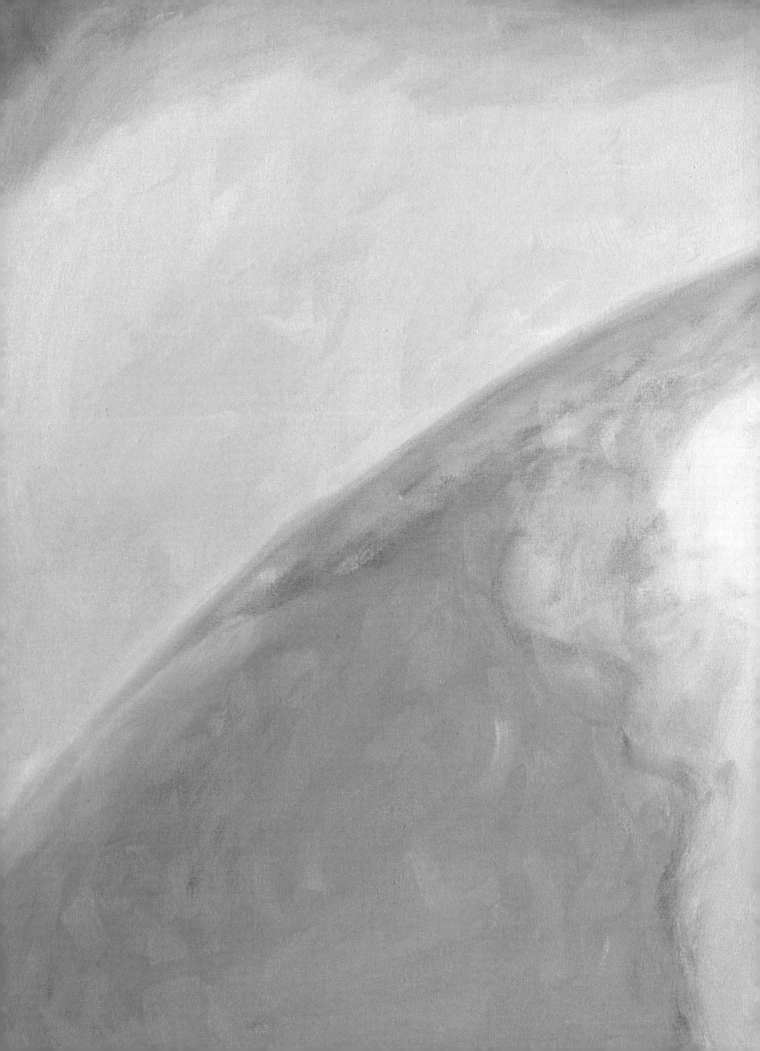

PEACE CRANE
SHEILA HAMANAKA

MORROW JUNIOR BOOKS
NEW YORK

*This poem is dedicated to the children
of Hiroshima and Nagasaki,
and to all children everywhere
who long for peace.*

Oil on canvas was used for the full-color illustrations.
The text type is 18-point Caxton Bold.

Copyright © 1995 by Sheila Hamanaka

Printed in the United States of America.

1 2 3 4 5 6 7 8 9 10

Library of Congress Cataloging-in-Publication Data
Hamanaka, Sheila.
Peace Crane / Sheila Hamanaka.
p. cm.
Summary: After learning about the Peace Crane, created by Sadako, a survivor of the bombing of Hiroshima, a young African American girl wishes it would carry her away from the violence of her own world.
ISBN 0-688-13815-2 (trade)—ISBN 0-688-13816-0 (library)
[1. Peace—Fiction. 2. Afro-Americans—Fiction.] I. Title. PZ7.H1692Pe 1995
[E]—dc20 95-1772 CIP AC

A CRANE FOR SADAKO

On August 6, 1945, the United States dropped an atomic bomb on Hiroshima, Japan. It was the first atomic bomb to be used on people. Three days later a second was dropped, on Nagasaki. It is impossible to know for sure, but estimates run as high as 250,000 dead and 100,000 wounded. Many of those who survived the burns from the flash continued to die from atomic radiation disease for years after World War II had ended.

Around the world people learned of the terrible suffering caused by this new bomb that could destroy a whole city in a single flash of fire. Many were touched by the story of Sadako Sasaki, who was just under two years old when the bomb fell on Hiroshima. She and most of her family survived. But ten years later, because she had been exposed to radiation, she was stricken with leukemia.

In Japan the crane is a symbol of long life, and it is said that if you fold a thousand paper cranes you will be granted your wish for health. Sadako folded a thousand cranes, and then even more. But on October 25, 1955, she died. Her classmates raised money for a monument that was built in her honor, and in memory of all the children who died because of the atomic bomb. People from all over the world still send thousands of paper cranes to be placed at the foot of Sadako's statue.

Peace Crane,
when the sun fell on Hiroshima,
you rose like a phoenix from the fire
and flew toward heaven in a flock.
Like a cloud,
a quarter million souls
went soaring up,
high above the heat,
high above the cries of war,
lifted by the love of those they left behind.

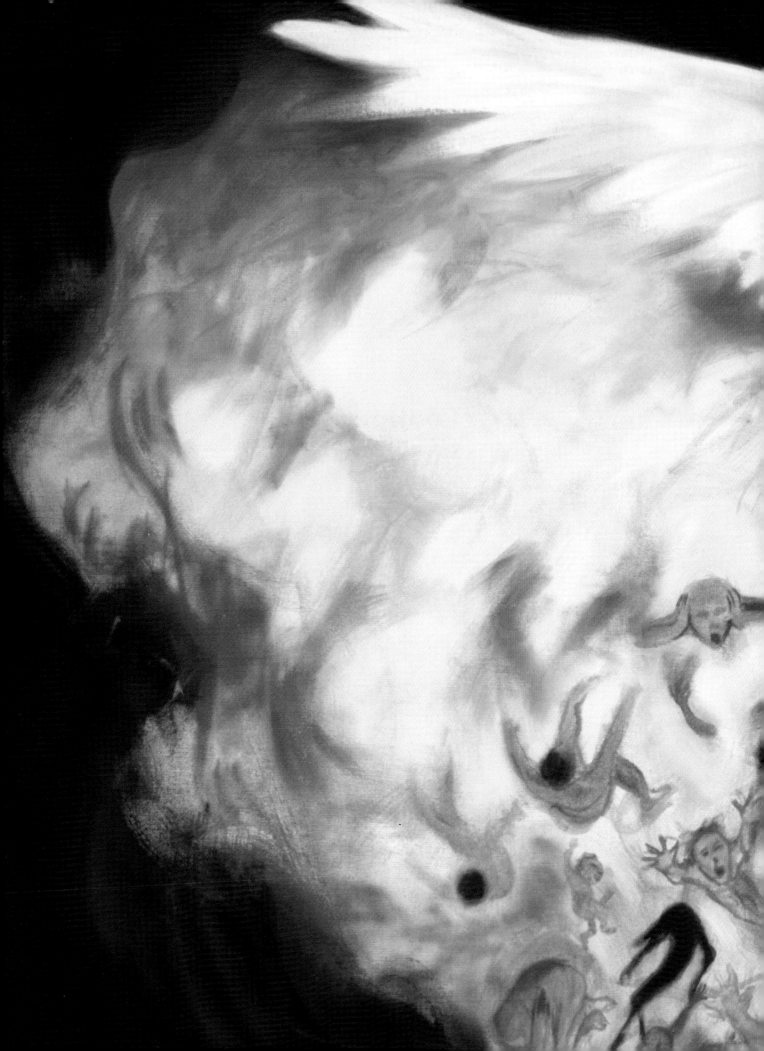

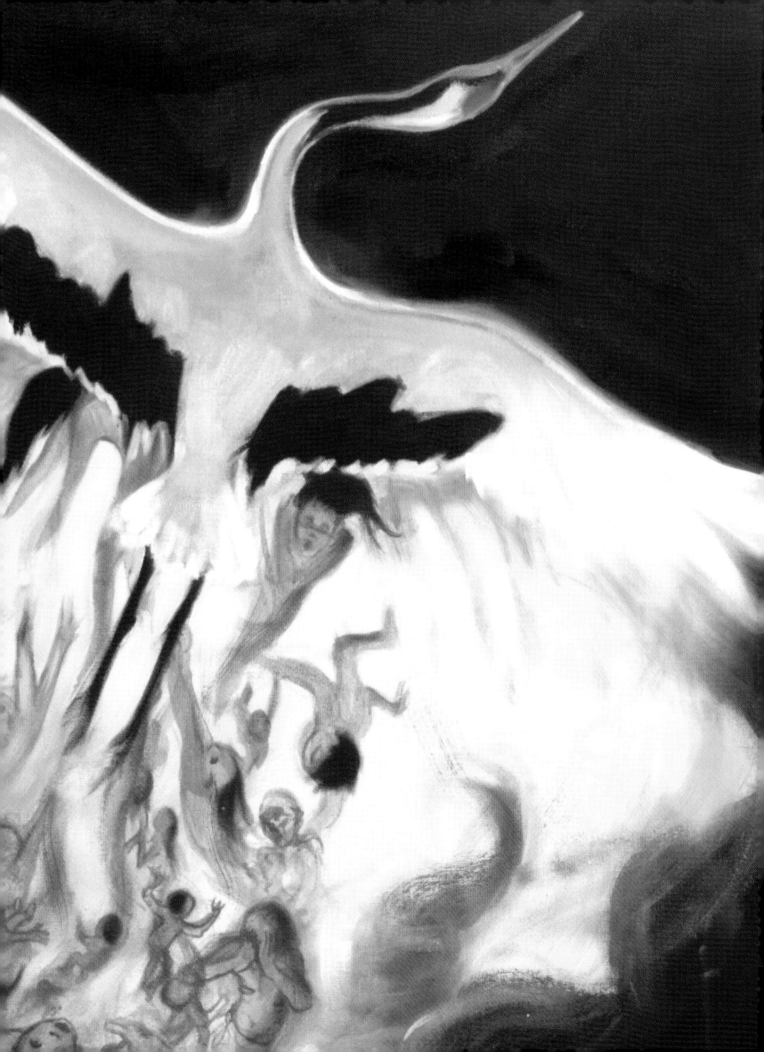

Peace Crane,
are you flying still?

My teacher says Sadako
folded a thousand paper cranes,
each one a tiny wish for life,
each one a wish for peace.

If I make a paper peace crane
from a crisp white paper square,
if I fold my dreams inside the wings,
will anybody care?

When the sun falls in the city,
when I hear shooting on my street,
I hold my ears and hope in my heart
that it's not a friend of mine.
Have their souls flown up to heaven?
Have a quarter million gone?
Sometimes I wonder, Peace Crane,
if I'm not far behind.

Peace Crane,
are you crying still?

You came for me, Peace Crane,
last night in a dream,
and we flew past golden mountains,
red rivers, forests green.

We flew so far to see the trees
that have lived for a thousand years,

and to listen to lullabies sung by whales
till our troubles disappeared.

We slipped past towns and farmland
—drifted from coast to coast—
and watched the sun set in the cities,
where we need you most.

I wanted to take you home with me,
I wanted you to stay.
I wanted to fold you in a dream
and tuck you safely away.

But deep inside I heard you saying,
in the deep blue of the night,
in the quiet whisper of your wings
on your ceaseless flight,

that your home is on this journey,
your home is in my heart,
your home is with the homeless,
who see you in the stars.

So fly, Peace Crane, fly,
fly as fast as you can.
If you come for me I'll follow,
but I'll know it's not a dream.
For now I remember
that I've seen you before....

I've seen you in the music
of my neighbor next door,

in the fluttering heartbeat
of a small bird set free,
and in songs sung by people
on the long road to peace.

We are rising to greet you,
Peace Crane, one by one.
We are soaring, many millions,
on a journey just begun.

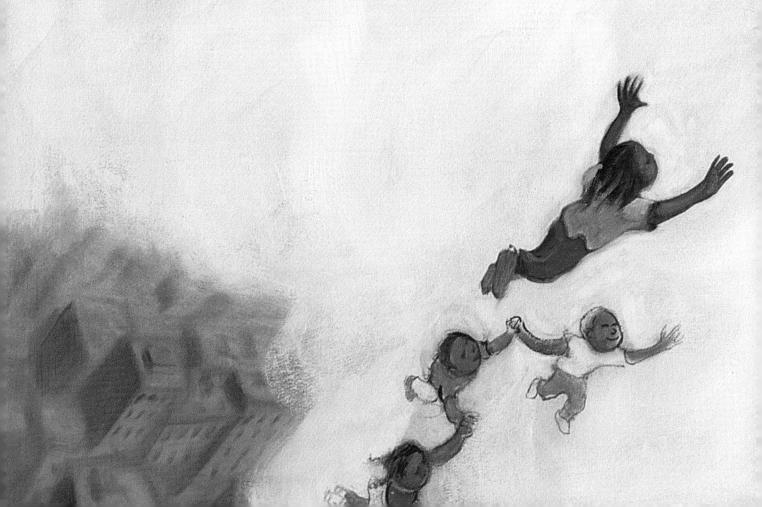

We will fly past Nagasaki,
and over Hiroshima,
until we finally see Sadako,
just as I've dreamed of her.
Now I can see her.
She's reaching toward the stars,
in a rainbow cloud of paper cranes
that have flown from near and far.

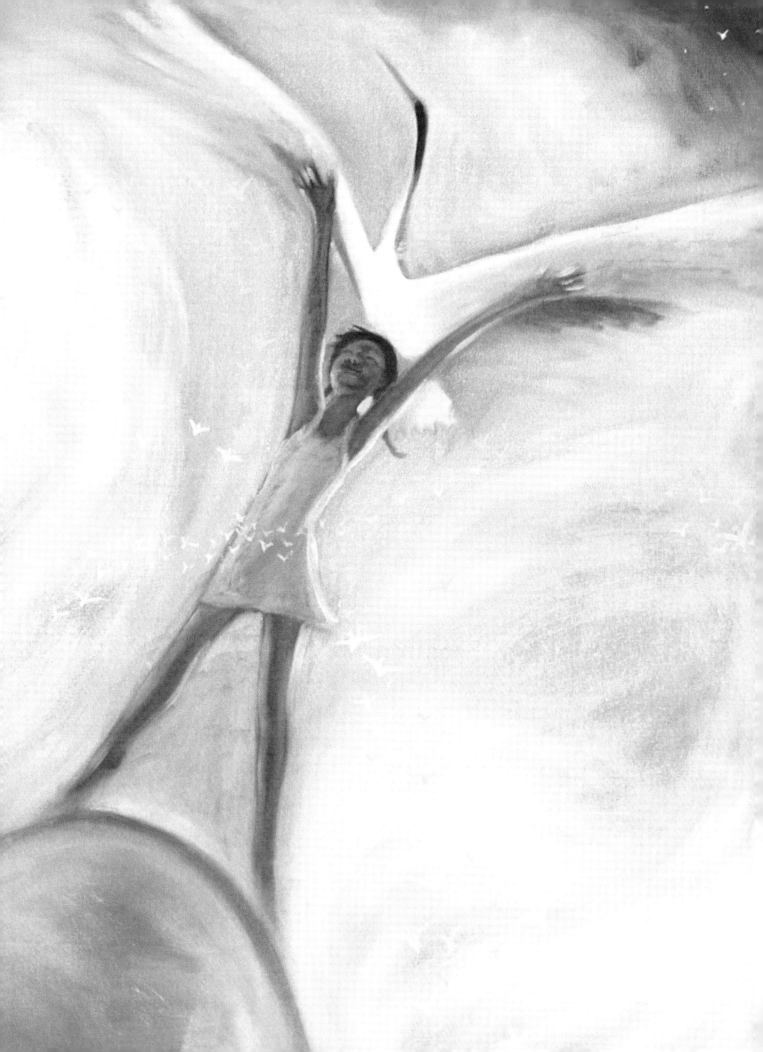

We have new voices, Peace Crane,
we have new hearts,
we have new eyes to see you with.
We long to be a part
of a world without borders,
of a world without guns,
of a world that loves its children,